A NOTE TO PARENTS

When your children are ready to "step into reading," giving them the right books—and lots of them—is as crucial as giving them the right food to eat. **Step into Reading Books** present exciting stories and information reinforced with lively, colorful illustrations that make learning to read fun, satisfying, and worthwhile. They are priced so that acquiring an entire library of them is affordable. And they are beginning readers with an important difference— they're written on four levels.

Step 1 Books, with their very large type and extremely simple vocabulary, have been created for the very youngest readers. **Step 2 Books** are both longer and slightly more difficult. **Step 3 Books,** written to mid-second-grade reading levels, are for the child who has acquired even greater reading skills. **Step 4 Books** offer exciting nonfiction for the increasingly proficient reader.

Children develop at different ages. **Step into Reading Books,** with their four levels of reading, are designed to help children become good—and interested—readers *faster*. The grade levels assigned to the four steps—preschool through grade 1 for Step 1, grades 1 through 3 for Step 2, grades 2 and 3 for Step 3, and grades 2 through 4 for Step 4—are intended only as guides. Some children move through all four steps very rapidly; others climb the steps over a period of several years. These books will help your child "step into reading" in style!

Library of Congress Cataloging-in-Publication Data
McMorrow, Catherine.
The jellybean principal / by Catherine McMorrow ; illustrated by Amy Wummer.
   p.   cm. — (Step into reading. Step 3 book)
SUMMARY: Jim, Ellen, and Judy see their friendship threatened when their uncontrollable
fighting in school gets them in trouble with the principal.
ISBN 0-679-84743-X (pbk.) — ISBN 0-679-94743-4 (lib. bdg.)
[1. Friendship—Fiction. 2. Schools—Fiction.] I. Wummer, Amy, ill. II. Title.
III. Series. PZ7.M478785Je 1994 [E]—dc20 93-26537

Manufactured in the United States of America   **12 11**

STEP INTO READING is a trademark of Random House, Inc.

Step into Reading™

THE JELLYBEAN PRINCIPAL

by Catherine McMorrow

illustrated by Amy Wummer

A Step 3 Book

Random House 🏠 New York

Judy was trying to listen to the teacher.
But Ellen said, "Do you have some paper?
Do you have a pencil?"

And Jim said, "Look at this!" He put his
ant farm in Judy's face. He pointed to an
ant. "She's the queen."

"Okay! Okay!" Judy said. She handed Ellen paper and pencil.

Mrs. Newit tapped the blackboard. "Let's talk about what ants do. Open your notebooks."

Judy opened her notebook. Just as she was starting to write, Jim dropped his ant farm on the floor.

"Clumsy!" Ellen said.

"Quit it!" Judy shouted.

Mrs. Newit laid down her ruler. "Judith Ann!" she called.

"Yes, ma'am." Judy stood up. *Crack!* She stood on the ant farm.

"It's not like you to be noisy, Judith," Mrs. Newit said.

"Ow!" Judy shouted.

"Excuse me?" said Mrs. Newit.

"Ow! Ow! OW!" Judy shouted.

"They're crawling up your legs!" screamed Ellen.

Jim took out his water pistols and started shooting at the ants.

Judy ran to Mrs. Newit. She jumped up and down and kicked wildly.

Mrs. Newit tried to brush the ants off Judy's legs. The ants bit her, too!

Jim ran up front, pistols squirting. He blasted Mrs. Newit.

"AAAAAACK!" she cried. "Help! Mr. Russo! Mr. Russo!"

The three friends sat in front of the principal's desk. On the desk was a bowl of jellybeans. Mr. Russo loved jellybeans. Kids did not get any.

"He certainly looks sour," Ellen whispered. "He probably thinks we are hooligans."

"Hooli-*whats?*" Jim hissed back.

"Bad guys," Judy explained. "Shhhh!"

Mr. Russo shook some jellybeans into his palm. He tossed one into his mouth. "Troublemakers, eh?" he said. He wrote their names on a piece of paper and pinned it to the wall.

Then he took a rag out of his drawer. He buffed his shoes.

The kids stared at him.

Mr. Russo looked up. "SCRAM!"

They took off like a shot! They ran across the playground and threw themselves against the fence.

Ellen grabbed Jim by the nose. "What's the big idea of using red biter ants? That's not *normal!*"

"Hey!" Jim said. "They're special from California!"

"So what?" Ellen stepped on Jim's

sneaker. "Where did you get your brain? Special from the moon?"

Judy turned away. "I'm going home! My bites hurt!"

Jim and Ellen ran to catch up.

"Guess what a red ant's favorite food is?" Jim asked.

"My ankles!" Judy answered.

"Nope," he said with a grin. "Jellybeans!"

The next day, Judy was trying to eat
lunch. Ellen kept bumping her. Jim kept
leaning over to steal her chips. "I'm
squished," she said.

"Look!" Ellen said, spitting crumbs. She pointed to her notebook. Jim had written on the cover:

I have a friend,
her name is Ellen.
She likes pie
and cheese and melon.
She is big and fat
and round.
Because she
eats them
by the pound!

"You call that poetry?" Judy said.

"Well, I was mad," Jim explained. "She cheated at Scrabble."

"I did not!" Ellen said.

"Don't start!" Judy told them. She threw a crumpled napkin at Jim. It missed and hit another boy. He threw back a raisin. The raisin whizzed past Judy's ear and hit another girl. She threw back a whole fistful of raisins.

"Wait!" Judy called. "It was an accident!"

But Ellen was glad. She just happened
to have a box of raisins in her pocket.

"Jim!" she said. "Look! Ammo!"
"No!" Judy shouted.
But in less than a minute
there was a storm of raisins.

Judy ducked under the table. "Old Jellybean will be here any minute," she thought. Then she noticed Jim and Ellen's sneakers. Quickly, she undid the laces and tied her friends to each other.

Once again, they ended up in front of the big desk.

Mr. Russo ate a jellybean and picked his teeth. He took out a red marker and stood up.

"NUM-BER TWO!" he growled. He marked a giant X over their names. He leaned over the desk and peered into their eyes.

"Next time, CONSEQUENCES!"

On the way home, Jim said, "What are 'CONSEQUENCES'?"

"I don't know," Ellen said. "But it can't be good."

"No kidding," Judy said. "And I missed violin practice, too."

"Don't be mad," Ellen pleaded.

"Let's forget about it," Jim said. "Come over and try my new scooter."

"Nope," said Judy. She wiped her glasses on her shirt. "I'm going home to read *Black Beauty*. Nice and quiet. No friends."

"Aw, come on," Jim said.

"Let her go," said Ellen. "You know Judith! A few hours of reading and she'll be good as new!"

The next day was sunny. Jim had his new scooter.

At recess they took turns doing figure eights around the swings and straightaways down the hill. Judy thought to herself, "It's good to have friends!"

But Ellen couldn't steer very well.

Jim yelled, "Turn! Turn!"

Ellen kept right on going. She ran into a mailbox.

Jim yelled, "Lookit! Look what you did! You're too fat to even steer!"

"She's not that fat," said Judy. "Don't be so mean." She ran to help Ellen. "What happened?" she asked. "Why did you close your eyes?"

Ellen was too dizzy to answer.

"Because she's a dumb chicken!" Jim yelled.

"Quit yelling!" Judy yelled. "Can't you see her knee is bleeding?"

"Her *kneeeee?*" Jim screamed. "What about my scooter! It's ruined! TOTALED!"

He marched over to Ellen's schoolbag. He took out her favorite book and tossed it down the sewer.

Judy bit her lip.

Ellen hopped up. "Okay! Put up your dukes!"

"Okay!" Jim said. "You big hippo!"

"Okay!" Ellen said. "Homely boy!"

Jim scooped up some dirt. "If you call someone a bad name, you ought to say a word they know, Scrabblehead!"

"Take it easy," Judy said. "Homely is just a fancy way to say ugly."

Jim looked wild.

"Uh-oh!" said Judy.

Jim rubbed dirt on Ellen's dress.

Ellen rubbed dirt in Jim's hair.

"You're even!" Judy said. "Now stop!"

"Not until he apologizes," Ellen said.

"Apologize? Me?" Jim said. "*You* broke my scooter. *You* should apologize."

"I didn't have a chance!" Ellen shouted. "You threw my book down the sewer!"

Ellen grabbed Jim's ear. She yanked on it with every word. "YOU–HAVE–A–TERRIBLE–TEMPER!"

"Yeow!" Jim hollered in pain. They started bonking each other on the head. Ellen missed Jim and hit Judy.

"My glasses!" Judy shouted. Just before they flew off her nose, she saw Old Jellybean. He was coming toward them. Fast.

"You're getting water on me," Ellen whispered to Jim. "Move over."

Jim dragged his bucket a little farther along the blackboard wall. He spilled soapy water on his shoe.

Judy sat on the other side of the room, sharpening pencils. Jim and Ellen could hear her grind a pencil, *chewwww,* then set it on the table, *click. Chewwww-click, chewwww-click.*

Mr. Russo came in. He wrote on the board.

Write 300 times:
I will not be an
instigator at
Pleasantville
School.

"That's not fair!" Judy said to herself. "I should write: I will not HANG AROUND with instigators."

"What's an instigator?" Jim asked.

"A person who stirs up trouble," Ellen explained.

"Hmmmmmm." Jim nodded.

Going home, Judy walked ahead. She could smell pencil on her fingers. "That's what I get for trying to keep the peace," she told herself.

Jim dragged his scooter. Ellen dragged herself. They were hot, sweaty, itchy, and unhappy.

Judy pretended she could not hear
the other two.

"Do you suppose she will still read to
us? Or let us swim in her pool?" Ellen
wondered. "Or watch her horse movies?
Or eat pie?"

Jim sighed. "Who knows? She may
even find new friends."

Ellen gasped. "Wait up!" she called out
to Judy.

But Judy kept walking.

Early the next morning,
Jim and Ellen baked
a cake. They took it
to school and set it
on Judy's desk.

Judy dumped it
in the trash can.

After school Jim and Ellen ran around
collecting gifts:

flowers

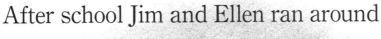

a homemade paper-clip dish

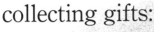

a plastic horse statue

eyeglass-cleaner towelettes
eyeglass strings
safety goggles

They left them
on Judy's porch.
Judy put them in a
paper bag and left the
bag on Jim's porch.

Then she watched a movie alone. She played hopscotch alone. She ate three large pieces of lemon pie, since she didn't have to share.

She lay on the couch. Suddenly, she heard a whooshing noise. A paper airplane flew through the window and landed on her face.

She opened it:

Dear Judith Ann,
Do you remember how we played games with you when you broke your leg? And how we bought you a scratching stick? Do you remember how we helped you learn your multiplication tables with horseshoes and apples? Do you remember how Jim threw away his lucky rabbit's foot because it gave you the creeps? You swore to be our friend forever! We're sorry and that's final! Totally sincerely,

James and
Ellen

Judy went to the window. "All right.
Come out wherever you are! I forgive you!"
Jim and Ellen jumped out of the
bushes.
"To the playground!" Jim shouted.

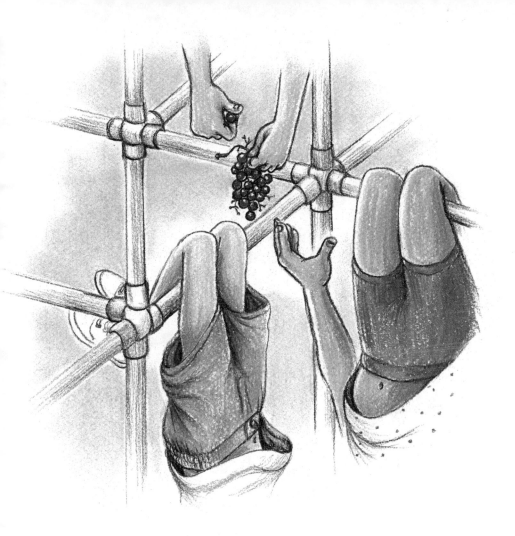

For a while they hung upside down on the monkey bars and ate grapes and talked.

Then Jim said, "Did you hear that?"

Ellen said, "It's somebody screaming."

They got down. They followed the noise to the door of the school.

Jim pressed his face to the glass. He pulled on the knob. Locked.

He went over to the basement window and jiggled it. "It's old," he said. He got a stick.

"What are you doing?" Ellen asked.

Jim worked at the window. "We're going in," he said.

"No," said Judy, backing away.

"No chance," said Ellen. "We're not allowed in the school after hours."

"Girls," Jim said, "there's a person inside who might be hurt."

Ellen sighed, then squeezed through the opening.

Judy followed. "It doesn't even sound like a person," she mumbled. "It sounds more like an animal."

They walked through the basement
and up to the cafeteria.

The noise was coming from the
cold-storage room. It was singing. Sort of.

"Row, row, row your boat
Over to the school.
Help, help, help, help,
I'm stuck inside the cooooool-er!
Hellllllp! Annnyyyybody! Please!"

It was Mr. Russo!

"Let's get out of here!" Judy hissed.

"I agree!" Ellen said. "We'll be expelled! Exiled! Banished!"

Jim looked at Ellen hard.

"Kicked out," Judy explained.

"*Helllllp!*" Mr. Russo called again.

Judy said, "Two against one, Jim." She and Ellen turned to go.

"He could die in there," Jim said.

Judy and Ellen stopped.

"Okay," Judy sighed.

"Heaven help us!" said Ellen.

They marched through the kitchen to
the cold-storage room.

"What's he doing in there, anyway?"
Judy wondered.

"Jellybeans!" said Jim. "He keeps them chilled in Baggies. Away from ants."

"OPEN THE DOOR!" Mr. Russo shouted.

"Yes, sir!" Jim grabbed a long spoon. He tried to pry open the door.

"We need help," Ellen said.

"The Fire Department!" Jim said. He dashed off.

"No! The police!" Judy called.

"COME BACK!" shouted Mr. Russo.

Ellen felt faint. She imagined herself in a prison uniform.

Jim found the fire-alarm box in the hall.
He pulled it.

BRRRRRRRRRRRRRRRRRRRING!

"JIIIIIM!" Ellen shouted. "We don't need
firemen! We need a locksmith!"

Soon they heard sirens. Ellen ran to the
window and looked out. Now, for sure,
they were going to jail.

"Oh no!" she cried. "Five fire engines for one principal!"

The firemen jumped off the trucks. They headed for the front door. A crowd had already gathered.

Jim ran to the window. They were about to chop the door down! He grabbed Judy. "Judy!" he shouted. "Judy! Judy!"

"Jim! Jim!" she shouted. "*What!*"

He pointed.

The firefighters lifted their axes. Jim and Judy flew down the hall to the door. Judy turned the latch. Jim pulled the bolt. They threw themselves against the door and swung it open.

"No!" they shouted. "There's no fire!"

In seconds Jim and Judy were racing back to the cafeteria. The fire chief, the police chief, the head of the school board, the mayor, a reporter, a photographer, and the fire crew all followed. They found Ellen sinking down in a corner. Judy and Jim pulled her up.

"Go ahead!" the mayor said. "Chop the door down!"

The firemen chopped. The door fell.

There sat Mr. Russo on a case of hot dogs. His skin was blue. His eyebrows were frosty. His teeth chattered. He had a jumbo bag of jellybeans on his lap.

"The red ones are my f-f-f-favorite," he said.

"What a great shot!" the photographer said. "Let's have the principal share his jellybeans with our three little heroes. All you chiefs gather round. Perfect!" *Snap.*

"Am I arrested?" Ellen asked. She rubbed her eyes.

Jim gave her a shove. "Smile, will you? They're taking your picture! You're a hero!"

"Heroine," Ellen said. "A female hero is a heroine."

"Whatever!" Judy said. She laughed and popped a jellybean in her mouth.